Colorful Journey

Written by

Jennifer Tiritilli Ranu

Giuliana Ranu and Karolina Ranu

To order additional copies of this book, contact:
Xlibris
1-888-795-4274
www.Xlibris.com
Orders@Xlibris.com

ISBN: 978-1-9845-7987-4 (sc)
ISBN: 978-1-9845-7988-1 (hc)
ISBN: 978-1-9845-7986-7 (e)

Library of Congress Control Number: 2020909428

Print information available on the last page

Rev. date: 07/21/2020

Colorful Journey

Written by
Jennifer Tiritilli Ranu
and
Giuliana Ranu and Karolina Ranu

Illustrated by
Caleigh Snyder
and
Giuliana Ranu

Contents

Chapter 1 Made in America! 1

Chapter 2 Fun and Games! 9

Chapter 3 What's his Name? 17

Chapter 4 You got It! 28

Chapter 5 It's for Real! 34

Acknowledgment

Giuliana Ranu and Karolina Ranu

I would like to thank my eleven-year-old twin granddaughters Giuliana Ranu and Karolina Ranu for coauthoring *Colorful Journey*. They each helped in providing detailed descriptions of the feelings children their age might encounter if confronted with the experiences presented to the children in *Colorful Journey*. Giuliana is an artist. She is a singer and plays the clarinet. Karolina is a pianist, and she loves to cook delicious recipes. Giuliana and Karolina have taken art classes at Lena Di Gangi Gallery in Totowa, New Jersey. They both take music lessons with Nancy Tiritilli. Giuliana and Karolina play basketball, soccer and have participated in swimming competitions. They performed at the Littleton School music concerts.

Caleigh Snyder

"Pictures speak louder than words!" I would like to thank Caleigh Snyder for providing the most clarifying illustrations that descriptively tell the exciting story, *Colorful Journey*. Caleigh Snyder, a young and talented illustrator, transformed words into beautiful images. She is a freshman, majoring in digital marketing at William Paterson University in New Jersey and has been working with various artistic programs that range from elementary school to high school. I wish Caleigh Snyder a colorful journey on the footpath to artistic success. Thank you! Thank you! Thank you!

CHAPTER 1

Made in America!

Dead-end Jersey Street at the foot of Garret Mountain in Paterson, New Jersey is a wonderful safe play street for children during the 1950s. This once cobblestone street has just been newly paved smooth black asphalt. I live in a two-family house with my African American family in a mostly Irish American and Italian American (Dublin section/ Little Italy section) neighborhood. When the bell rings after the neighborhood kids and I spend a long hot day in the classrooms at School No. 3 on Main Street, and whenever we walk home from school a few blocks up the hill of dead-end Jersey Street, surely our salivary glands turn on high. The tasty smells of fried chicken puff out of the open windows of my house and the spicy aroma of corned beef and cabbage, or spaghetti and meatballs drift out of our neighbors' open windows. Delicious! *Mmmmmmmmmmm!* My family and friends call me Sweety. Dad tells me that I'm an ever-sweet chocolate chip cookie!

There is little fear of much street traffic in the 1950s in Paterson, New Jersey, unless you walk to the business district Downtown. Here, not just cars but busses and trucks travel to the stores and movie theaters that line both sides of Main Street and Market Street. Mom holds my hand every Saturday as we cross the streets and walk to shop Downtown at S. S. Kresge's, a ¢5 and ¢10 store. My stay-at-home mom spends many hours almost every day in the kitchen at the stove cooking homemade delights for our family. She is a great baker of cookies, sweet chocolate chip cookies! Lots of Mom's time is also spent washing dirty clothes in a ringer washing machine. Then, she hangs the clean wet items with wooden clothespins to dry on a clothesline rope that runs over a pulley hooked outside of the kitchen window and runs to another pulley that is attached to a tall apple tree in our backyard. Since clothes dryers have not been introduced in my neighborhood yet, almost every backyard on dead-end Jersey Street in the 1950s looks like mine. They display wet clothes hanging on a clothesline to dry. That is one reason why Mom and all of my friends' moms love clear skies and sunny days.

Dad works as a carpenter in construction, building structures throughout Passaic County in New Jersey. We are considered to be very lucky. Only a few families that live on dead-end Jersey Street own a car. Dad drives a green 1957 Plymouth station wagon that is perfect for carrying his carpenter's tools to the construction worksite and for transporting our family wherever, if it is not within walking distance.

Paterson's textile industry has blossomed and grown over the years. There are many factories and mills located on the streets down the hill at the foot of Garret Mountain in Paterson, New Jersey. In fact, one of the streets in this neighborhood is named Mill Street. Most of my friends' parents are factory workers. Every day, moms and dads walk to and from their place of work at the *Sweatshops* a few blocks from where I live. *Sweatshops*! There is no air-conditioning! The heat buildup from the working machines in the huge red-brick factories makes the factory working space's inner surroundings very hot and uncomfortable, especially during the summer.

As time has moved on, in addition to the textile industry, new inventions have been created throughout the city of Paterson, New Jersey. Locomotive engines, airplane parts, automobile paint, pipe organs, nail polish, and many other today products are manufactured in Paterson's factories where our grandparents and parents are working in the 1950s.

Who made this happen? Why? When?

In 1775–1783, George Washington, who served as commander-in- chief of the Continental Army during the Revolutionary War and as the first President of the United States, spent much time at the vicinity of the Passaic River near his headquarters at the Dey Mansion in Preakness Valley/Wayne, New Jersey. He very often galloped on his horse about Preakness Valley throughout a wild mountainous, wooded area that led to a winding freshwater river and great, thunderous massive waterfalls. On July 10, 1778, knowing that much power could be harnessed from this flowing river great waterfalls, George Washington, Alexander Hamilton, and Marquis de Lafayette parked their horses near a huge granite rock at the bank of this flowing river. They relaxed to have a picnic lunch and talk about the industrial future of this new independent productive nation. At this time and place, they envisioned and discussed how this, great thunderous massive waterfalls could provide much energy to power the machines in the new factories and mills that would be built along this flowing river. These Founding Fathers had the foresight to predict that huge factories and mills built here would manufacture many products that had been previously purchased from and taxed by England.

Great Falls!   Water Wheels!

Turbines!   Power!

So, what do you think they ate for lunch? This winding fresh water river was full of catfish or sunfish, and the wild wooded tree area surrounding the great massive waterfalls provided shelter for lots of birds and other wild animals like groundhogs, rabbits, and deer. Dad told me that while sitting on the ground to picnic, George Washington, Alexander Hamilton, and Marquis de Lafayette ate animal's tongue roasted on an open fire and placed on crunchy biscuits. *Yummmmmmmmmmm!* There were no Libby's hotdogs in this neighborhood in those days!

The first President of the United States, George Washington served two terms as president, 1789–1797. Alexander Hamilton served as Secretary of the Treasury, and in 1792 the investment group Society of Useful Manufacturers (SUM) was established in Paterson to reduce this new nation's dependence on foreign goods. Pierre L'Enfant, a civil engineer, designer of Washington DC, also designed a raceway system with three tiers and man-made waterfalls to generate more power for this industrial city. Paterson became known as the Silk City.

Paterson, New Jersey!   Made in America! YEAH!

Over the years in 1800s and 1900s, Paterson's booming manufacturing industry offered much work for immigrants, who traveled for weeks by boat to cross the vast Atlantic Ocean from countries in Europe. These European immigrants left behind their familiar homeland. They came to a new unfamiliar land to settle and work. Their exhausting arrival to Ellis Island was brightened with the expectation of living in this promising country, the United States of America. Many European immigrants came to settle in Paterson, New Jersey, with a wish to make a better life for themselves and for their families. At the neighboring flowing river and great waterfall area, many people including children worked in huge red-brick factories and mills throughout the city for twelve to fifteen hours a day and seven days a week. Many were employed to work in these *Sweatshops* as a weaver, dyer to color fabrics, or as a seamstress to sew the fabric to make clothing. Sometimes, children could only see their daddy on Sunday when their mom set up a picnic and the family met daddy at the factory grounds for lunch.

Not everyone's parent in my neighborhood worked in a factory. There were diverse types of work in Paterson. Some immigrants worked long days in strenuous construction. There were no bulldozers in those days. With a pick and shovel, many men dug the hard, earthy rock ground to place the foundations for the building of structures, like beautiful churches, schools, stores, and huge red-brick factories throughout this booming industrial city, Paterson, New Jersey.

Enough was enough! Italian immigrants, Maria and Pietro Botto came to America in 1892 from Biella, Italy. Pietro and his wife moved to Norwood Street in Haledon, New Jersey, in 1908. Pietro Botto was a silk mill worker. After a long day at work or on the weekends, many laborers met under the shade of the green leaves of the grapevine or to play bocci at Maria and Pietro Botto's backyard. Maria served delicious home-cooked meals to the laborers as discussions centered around unfavorable, exhausting working conditions in the factory workplaces throughout the industrial city of Paterson. The Botto House became a frequent meeting place for laborers' assembly and free speech. The Industrial Workers of the World (IWW) union leaders spoke from the second-floor front balcony of the Botto House to nearly 20,000 factory workers. In 1913 the Paterson Silk Strike resulted. Many factory workers united by going on strike. They stopped working the production of goods, causing the fall of Paterson's textile industry. This protest successfully made many changes for better working conditions that included an eight-hour workday.

Made in America, the beautiful!

CHAPTER 2

Fun and Games!

I wonder what kind of games kids played in the days when George Washington was here in the vicinity of the Passaic River and Garret Mountain? There is no way that they could have played the same fun games my friends and I play in the 1950s.

During every season, kids from neighboring streets throughout Paterson, New Jersey, come to play outdoors on dead-end Jersey Street at the foot of Garret Mountain. We play by bright sunlight during the day, and telephone-pole streetlight in the early evening. When school is out for summer break and the hot July sun beats down on thirsty game-playing kids, drops of sweat drip off our foreheads to sizzle and evaporate upon contact with the surface of the hot asphalt street. *Szzzzzzzzzzzz*!

During spring and summer, neighborhood kids enjoy the exciting acceleration of roller-skating down dead-end Jersey Street's hill or playing roller-skate tag. *Weeeeeee!*

You're it! We wear metal roller skates that need a skate key to make adjustments for a proper fit onto our feet, wearing leather shoes. To avoid losing our ever-precious skate key, kids wear the metal skate key dangling on a white, black, or brown shoelace tied around their necks like a necklace. If we lose our skate key, we might be in big trouble. It will be very difficult to detach our metal roller skates from our shoes without tearing off the hard leather shoe soles without a skate key. Precious skate key! How do we stop roller-skating? We crash-fall onto the concrete sidewalk or the hard street pavement. Sometimes we could stop roller-skating by colliding into the big green garage doors at the corner of Jersey Street. *Boooooom!* No, we do not wear helmets or kneepads.

Hopscotch anyone? All we need is a rubber-shoe heel and a piece of white chalk.

Sneakers are only allowed to be worn in school for gym class (physical education) in the 1950s. There is always constant walking in shoes to and from school on the concrete sidewalks, walking to shop at the neighborhood grocery stores, to the movie theaters or shopping in the stores in Downtown Paterson, and walking to visit Hinchliffe Stadium to see a sporting event. People walk to church, to the parks, to the workplace, or to visit friends. This causes many to wear out their shoes' soles or heels. Shoe repairs could be made at Dan's Shoemaker Shop on Grand Street in Paterson, New Jersey. Dan the Shoemaker always gives us a few worn-out rubber heels from men's shoes to throw into the numbered boxes when we play hopscotch. Dan the Shoemaker also repairs the soles that are torn off when someone tries to get their roller skates off without using their skate key.

A piece of white chalk! There is always at least one piece of white chalk missing from the blackboard chalk ledge in the classrooms throughout the school district in the city of Paterson. Ask any teacher who teaches here in the 1950s, especially at School No. 3. Teachers have lots of only white chalk to write on the classroom slate blackboards, so they often give kids a piece of white chalk if they ask and say, "Please." With the white chalk, we draw and number the hopscotch rectangular boxes from 1 to 9 and the HOME box on the sidewalk or on the street.

The neighborhood boys play stickball in the middle of dead-end Jersey Street. This game is similar to playing baseball except for a few things. For a bat, all the boys need is mom's old wooden broomstick. They cut off the worn flat bristles of the broom and use the wooden broomstick as a bat. The rubber ball is a pink *Spaldeen, Spalding High Bouncer.* They play in the street, so the home plate is the metal manhole cover in the middle of the street. First base is the telephone pole. Second base is the other manhole in the street opposite the home plate, and third base is the bright-red fire hydrant that stands at the broken concrete sidewalk in front of my house. If a boy hits the ball into the empty, abandoned land across the street from my house, the Old Lots, it's a foul ball! If the *Spaldeen* is hit-smacked up the street to the first tier of Garret Mountain, it is a homerun! *SMACK!*

There are no supermarkets in my neighborhood in the 1950s. I am one of those kids, who rides my purple two-wheeler bike to Dinah's Corner Store to buy a five-cent bag of potato chips, pretzels, or some sweet penny candy. Mom often sends me to Dinah's Corner Store to buy a loaf of bread and perhaps a half pound of bologna so she could make lunch sandwiches for my always-hungry brother, Peanut, and me. Between the handlebars of my bike is a metal basket that securely holds the brown paper bag with the purchased bread and bologna. I usually eat the potato chips, pretzels, or candy before I pedal pump my bike up Jersey Street's hill to bring the package home to Mom. *Lunch! Uhhhhhhhhh!*

The Fourth of July is a great day on dead-end Jersey Street at the foot of Garret Mountain. Neighbors celebrate Independence Day to pay tribute to our Founding Fathers for all that they did to establish this amazing country, the United States of America, and for their determination in making Paterson this wonderful city that we know. Holding and waving glittering silver sparklers, dazzling the darkness in the night, kids call out, "George Washington! My hero!" Fire crackers thrown in the air by neighborhood boys, who place them in an empty tin can to explode in the middle of the street is very excitingly dangerous. Many people sit on a bed blanket covering hard dirt ground at the first tier of Garret Mountain or on homemade splintery hard wooden benches that they drag from under their backyards' grapevines to the middle of dead-end Jersey Street. Here, they watch the spectacular fireworks display that is projected from the amazing arena at Hinchliffe Stadium in Paterson, New Jersey. The nighttime sky becomes magically illuminated. Red! White! Blue! *Boooom !*

Bangggggggggggggggg! *Boooom !* We all clap and yell, *"YEAH !"*

During autumn, when the green leaves of the tall trees that tower Garret Mountain turn to crinkle orange, yellow, and red, the neighborhood boys play touch football—not tackle—right in the middle of dead-end Jersey Street. Great long passes thrown by the quarterback are caught, and the receiver runs to the goal line to score. Sometimes the boys play flag football. It is almost the same game, but they place a red handkerchief in the pants' back pocket of the boy who catches the football, and instead of tackling him, a boy on the other team pulls the red handkerchief out of the football carrying boy's pocket. This prevents a hard-crash collision with Jersey Street's surface. The neighborhood girls and I shout loudly as we cheer for the boys at the sidewalk in front of my house. *"Junior! Junior! He's our man!*

T-E-A-M, Yeah . . . TEAM ! T-E-A-M, Yeah . . . TEAM!"

There is cold, cold fun in the winter. When the black asphalt-paved Jersey Street surface and the three tiers of Garret Mountain are puffy white snow covered, it is fun for kids! Whenever it snows, every tree branch, sidewalk, front step, cellar door, or parked car on dead-end Jersey Street in the 1950s is covered white. Sometimes there are one, two, or three feet of snow that settles on the ground in our neighborhood! No school!

Snow day! Kids anxious to play in the snow, dress wearing warm winter snowsuits, homemade colorful crochet hats, scarfs and mittens, and rubber snow boots. My rubber snow boots are red. It is lots of fun rolling cold, icy snow to make snowballs. The neighborhood kids throw snowballs at each other when we have a snowball fight.

We love rolling snow to make three large snowballs to create at least one snowman in someone's snow-covered backyard or front yard. Dressing the snowman is fun too. Someone always has grandpa's old hat to place on the snowman's icy cold head.

The most winter fun that I enjoy is sleigh riding on a flat metal sled from the first tier of Garret Mountain down the steep snow-covered Jersey Street hill. Sometimes, kids play sleigh ride train. The train engine leader kid lies down prone on the first sled. Another kid does the same but holds onto the first kid's rubber-booted feet. The third kid or the caboose, lying prone on his or her sled, holds onto the second kid's feet. Push! *Weeeeeeeeeeeee!* It is almost always a breathtakingly, shivering fun experience to sleigh ride like a moving train down Jersey Street's steep hill. Almost always! To stop or avoid crossing the intersection of Jersey Street and Slater Street, kids often steer their sleds into the same green garage doors that stopped them from roller-skating.

Brrrrrr! Boooom !

In the summer, autumn, winter, or spring, kids play many different types of games outdoors in the middle of dead-end Jersey Street at the foot of Garret Mountain. There are rules for the games that most kids follow. We play many more fun games in the 1950s in the middle of dead-end Jersey Street. So, I wonder! I kind of figure that the types of fun games that kids played in the days when George Washington was here were probably Hide-and-Seek and Tag. The vicinity of the Passaic River and this Garret Mountain area has many tall trees and boulder rocks that those kids could hide behind. There is also a lot of open space to play Tag! You're it!

CHAPTER 3

What's his Name?

My good friends are ten-year-old twins, artistic Giuliana and timid, shy Karolina. They live in a cute house up the street from my house on dead-end Jersey Street. A tall maple tree's stretching branches and beautiful green leaves cast a delightful shady shadow over the steps that lead to the front door of their house. On warm weekend days or whenever there is no school, this place is where most of the dead-end Jersey Street neighborhood kids like to hang out to cool off in the shade after playing fun games. It is where artistic, Giuliana can be found sitting on the top step at the front stoop most of the day, gazing at the majestic colorful mountain with either a colorful crayon, pencil, or paintbrush in her hand. Neighborhood kids love to listen to Giuliana softly sing, "Garret Mountain", as she draws wonderful pictures with crayons on a sketchpad that she always carries with her.

Garret Mountain

Garret Mountain touching the sky,
Puffy white clouds and birds flying by,
Little children dance at your feet,
Playing hopscotch and stickball on Jersey Street.
I'm so lucky that I found,
A Garret Mountain with a crown.

Garret Mountain green with your trees,
Golden buffalo grass sways in the breeze,
Wild clover, the watering spring,
Here comes the train. Let it sing. Let it sing.

Garret Mountain majestic castle and pond,
Just as it is with the wave of a wand,
Make it happen, a shimmering glow,
Sleigh riding down your steep hills of white snow.

I'm so lucky that I found,
A Garret Mountain with a crown.

I love to play hopscotch and roller-skate on metal skates that need a skate key with Giuliana, Karolina, and our great friend JoAnne. We often jump rope with a piece of an old clothesline rope on the uneven bumpy sidewalk or on the slick paved surface in the front of our houses on dead-end Jersey Street. Karolina just likes to be a steady ender! Jump! Jump! Jump! I taught all my friends how to jump, *Double- Dutch*!

Standing at the sidewalk in front to my house holding a rubber-shoe heel in one hand and a jump rope in the other, Karolina calls to Giuliana, who is sitting in her usual spot at the stoop in front of her house, "Want to play hopscotch with us? We'll let you be first." Then, I call out to Giuliana, "Don't throw the rubber-shoe heel on the line. You're gonna be fine." JoAnne shouts, "Don't step on the line. You're gonna be fine!" Giuliana does not respond. She holds onto her sketchpad and cardboard box of colorful crayons, sits very still, and continues to gaze up at Garret Mountain that appears to Giuliana to be within an arm's reach in front of her. Karolina, JoAnne, and I walk up the street to meet Giuliana. As I lean on the dry, rough dark-gray bark of the maple tree's trunk, I ask, "Would you rather play jump rope with us? We'll be the enders." Karolina says, "Jump in on time. You're gonna be fine!" Giuliana looks up, ignoring our invitations to play. It is like she is in a fog—a hazy-gray daze. I'm beginning to think she has snapped!

Giuliana, paying no attention to us, slowly descends the front steps of her house and begins to walk as though she is in a trance, holding onto her sketchpad and colorful crayons. Slowly, she leaves the front stoop at her house and begins to walk up dead-end Jersey Street to a winding footpath that seems to lead to the first tier of this magically colorful pine-green Garret Mountain. Karolina calls to her sister, "Giuliana! Giuliana!" There is no response from Giuliana. Karolina throws the hopscotch rubber heel and old clothesline jump rope onto the hard ground surface and chases after, to join her twin sister. She calls out, "Wait for me. Where are you going?" Then from under the shade of the tall maple tree, I call both of them, "Wait for us!" JoAnne and I run up the steep Jersey Street hill to catch up with Karolina and Giuliana. *Pufffffff* !

Giuliana walks softly toward a patch of dazzling wild purple clover that lines on both sides of the winding footpath in Garret Mountain. She begins picking a bunch of puffy purple clover flowers to make a dainty handful bouquet. Karolina, JoAnne, and I, out of breath from running up the hill to catch up with Giuliana, begin to pick the pretty purple flowers too. Giuliana puts the freshly picked bouquet to her nose, inhales deeply to smell the lovely sweet purple flower's fragrance. *Ummmmmmmmmm!* Then before we know it, she tosses the puffy purple flowers bouquet over her head several feet into the bright sunshine and open air. As the dainty purple flowers float gently and silently to the ground, something else suddenly, suddenly moving catches Karolina's eyes.

Timid, shy Karolina looks up in amazement and takes a very deep breath as a big, plump, fluffy, butternut yellow groundhog scampers over to us and boldly roars, "Hay! This is my territory. My clover! My mountain! What are you doing here, intruders?" Shockingly to us, Giuliana responds to the groundhog in a stern voice, "Intruders! Oh no. I am following this winding footpath." Karolina says, "I'm following her." JoAnne and I reply, "We are too!" Then Giuliana, speaking directly to the groundhog asks, "Do you know where this winding footpath goes?" The groundhog replies, "Of course I know where it goes. This is my territory. My clover! My mountain! Why should I tell you where it goes? You don't belong here!" Giuliana firmly answers, "Oh, but we do. We are Jersey girls. My sister, Karolina and I live in a cute little house on Jersey Street, just at the foot of this beautiful colorful mountain. Our friends, JoAnne and Sweety live in houses on Jersey Street too. Every day and night, I look out my bedroom's glassy window and gaze at this beautiful Garret Mountain. By the moonlight, I wish on a twinkling bright shining star that sits in the dark blue night sky just above the third tier of this mountain, and by the sun's daylight, I sit on the top step of the stairs at the front stoop of my house to sketch things that I see in this colorful majestic Garret Mountain. I love to draw . . . love . . . love the colors of this mountain. I love to see the white of winter turn to shades of green in the spring, and the burst of vibrant summer turns to the mellow orange and yellow colors of autumn on this colorful mountain. And . . . then there is the start of this winding footpath? I wonder, where does it go? Does it lead to colorful wonder? Can you tell me where it goes?"

The big, plump, fluffy, bossy groundhog replies, "This is my territory. This is my home!" As he points to a red robin, a tan deer, and a brownish-gray rabbit nibbling on the purple flowers of the wild clover, the groundhog says, "These are my friends." Very politely, Giuliana asks the groundhog, "Can I be your friend?" Simultaneously Karolina, JoAnne, and I say, "Us too?" Then, we begin to sing "I'm Your Friend" as we hold hands and happily dance about the patch of beautiful, wild purple clover.

I'm Your Friend

I'm your friend, I'm your friend,
I want to be there, whenever you need me,
I'm your friend, I'm your friend, I'm your friend.

I'm your friend, I'm your friend,
Every time you call, I'll come a-running,
I'm your friend, I'm your friend, I'm your friend.

I'm your friend, I'm your friend,
Loyal, honest, buddies till the end,
Stay with me. I'll always be your friend.

As we conclude singing "I'm Your Friend" and take a curtsy bow, there is huge applause and happy roars from all the groundhog's animal friends. Even a few more animal friends hiding behind the bushes join in the cheering. After the applause settles down, the groundhog slowly replies directly to Giuliana, "Okay! Okay! I'll make a deal with you. You have one day. If you can guess my name, the name my mother gave me at birth, not the name my friends call me . . . I will lead you on an amazing colorful journey that follows this winding footpath from one end of Garret Mountain to the other end. Giuliana, . . . bring your sketchpad, Karolina, JoAnne, Sweety, and some of your other friends. Same place, same time . . . tomorrow. Guess my name!"

Giuliana is beamingly excited to have this opportunity. She smiles and says, "Oh yes! Guess your name. Please give me a hint!" As the groundhog begins to run off with the other animals into the pine-green mountain's camouflage, he calls out, "Colorful journeyyyyyyyyyyyyyy!"

What a day! I can't wait to tell all my friends on Jersey Street about our encounter with the big, plump, fluffy, bossy groundhog. It is late afternoon and the dead-end Jersey Street kids are still up to their usual activities of playing games, roller-skating, and riding their bikes on the street. But when we come down from the first tier of this three-tier mountain, backtracking on the footpath, the four of us return to sit on the front steps at the stoop of Giuliana and Karolina's house. Here we can enjoy the cool, refreshing breeze generated by the moving green leaves of the tall maple tree and try to sort out what has just happened. Giuliana looking extremely puzzled and sounding supper sad, asks, "*Ummmmm*! How can I know that groundhog's real name? I don't even know what his friends call him!"

A delightfully beautiful blue dragonfly gracefully lands on the hard, wooden banister railing at the front steps, and a red robin flies in to greet us. The red robin walks a few steps on the earthy dirt ground below us. Giuliana takes a few colorful crayons out of her crayon box and begins to make a drawing in her sketchpad of the blue dragonfly and the red robin. Karolina, very softly speaks to the blue dragonfly and the red robin, "Beautiful blue dragonfly and red robin, is the big, plump, fluffy groundhog that hangs out by the footpath in the mountain your friend?" They both look at her. She continues. "Do you know his real name?" The beautiful blue dragonfly flutters her lacy wings and says, "*Hmmmm*, I call my groundhog friend, Big Guy." The red robin twitches up his head and says, "He is my friend. I call him, Leader." Karolina blinks her eyes and shakes her head to reply, "Oh, I don't think his mother would have named her baby groundhog, Big Guy or Leader. Thanks anyway." Then, as both of the groundhog's friends fly away, Giuliana holds up the sketches she has just created of the beautiful blue dragonfly and the red robin. I think, "Such detail! Talent! Wow! Giuliana is such an artist!"

Karolina repeats, "*Hmmmmmmm*. Colorful journey?" She turns to her sister and suggests, "Why don't you draw a picture of that big, plump, fluffy, bossy groundhog? Anyway, if you don't know his real name, perhaps by presenting him with a fantastic picture of himself, he will still lead us on an amazing colorful journey across the winding footpath through Garret Mountain." Giuliana takes a few seconds to think about her sister's proposal and then she replies, "Good idea, Karolina. I will get started on drawing a picture of the groundhog right now."

I love to watch Giuliana draw, so I sit very quietly on the second step at the stoop as she begins to transform a blank sheet of white paper in her sketchpad into a very handsome facsimile of this big, plump, fluffy, bossy groundhog. Giuliana sits on the top step and continues to draw. As she reaches for a crayon, the cardboard crayon box falls over and some of the waxy crayons begin to roll down the steps. The sound echoes,

"Drrrr . . . dip . . . dop. Drrrr . . . dip, dip . . . dop . . . drrrr!" as the waxy crayons fall and roll. Karolina, JoAnne, and I hurry off the steps to retrieve them for fear that these colorful crayons might continue to roll down the steep Jersey Street hill. One by one, we pick up all the rolling crayons and stuff them back into the cardboard crayon box. Karolina comments, *"Hmmmmmmm.* Colorful journey?" She holds one crayon at a time between her fingers and softly reads the name of the color that is printed on the paper wrapper surrounding the waxy crayon. "Burnt-orange . . . Blue-gray . . . Tan-thistle . . . Lavender-pink . . . Brick-red . . . Butternut-yellow." Giuliana jumps off the top step of the stoop and yells out loud, "That's it! Give me that crayon, please. Butternut-yellow is the perfect color that I need for this groundhog's fluffy coat!"

Then a few cute neighborhood boys, riding their bikes to the front steps at the stoop, come to greet us. A few seconds later, just behind them, other friends with metal skate keys dangling on old shoelaces from around their necks, roller-skate to the maple tree to hang out in the shade with us. My brother Peanut says, "Hi. What are you doing?" Karolina shyly points up the street to the footpath and explains, "This morning, we took a walk on the winding footpath. We met a big, plump, fluffy, bossy groundhog that hangs out there. He made a deal with Giuliana. If she can guess his real name, he will lead us on an amazing colorful journey on the winding footpath across Garret Mountain. Giuliana is preparing a sketch of the groundhog to offer in case she does not know his real name." That's when I jump in and ask my brother Peanut and our other friends, "You wouldn't happen to know that groundhog's real name, would you?"

Dom, a bike-riding boy replies, "I've seen that plump, bossy groundhog hanging around the Old Lots nibbling on the wild purple clover and yellow dandelions' flowers near the footpath. One time I threw a rock at an old metal street sign at the sidewalk by Dinah's Corner Store and the loud *Bonggggggggggg* sound made that groundhog run away very fast. Sorry though, I don't know his real name." Junior, a roller-skating friend comments as he rolls on metal wheels around the giant maple tree, "One day I saw that groundhog near the footpath, I don't know his real name either, but as I began singing, "See You in September," I could swear that he stood up on his hind legs and clapped his paws for me. What a happening!"

Rachel, another roller-skating friend says, "Our roller skates' metal wheels make a deafening sound as we skate on the paved street or concrete sidewalk. It scares him away. I don't know his real name either." They all laugh when Nancy, another friend on roller skates says, "One day, I tried to call him, Here boy! Here boy! He just took off like lightning. I wish I knew his real name." All our friends agree that they are aware of this groundhog, but they don't know the groundhog's real name. Then Nancy and Junior began to sing, "What's His Name?"

What's His Name?
What's his name? What's his name?
He just likes to play this game.
What's his name? What's his name?
Does it give him any fame?
Hope very soon we'll claim,
Winners of this game.

Does this mountain know why?
As it touches the sky,
We need to name this guy.
What's his name? What's his name? What's his name?

Giuliana invites our friends as the groundhog has suggested, "Would you like to come along with us tomorrow to meet the big, plump, fluffy, bossy groundhog?" They reply, "Sure. See you tomorrow." As Peanut and Dom pick up the kickstands of their two-wheeler bikes and ride away down Jersey Street's hill, Dom calls out, "Colorful journeyyyyyyyyyyyyyyyyyy!" Junior, Nancy, and Rachel roller-skate down the steep Jersey Street hill, creating a roaring, thunderous sound as the metal wheels of their skates sang out in unison. *Rooooooooooooooooooooooool!* Giuliana closes her sketchpad and she picks up the cardboard box of waxy crayons. Karolina opens the big front door of their house. They bade farewell as they both walk indoors. JoAnne says, "Good-bye." I say, "See you tomorrow." As I slowly walk on the sidewalk to my home down Jersey Street's hill, I am thinking, "Colorful journeyyyyyyyyyyyyyyyyy! What is that big, plump, fluffy, bossy groundhog's real name?"

CHAPTER 4

You got It!

The next morning, as the beaming sun peeks through the slats of the metal blinds on the glassy bedroom windows, Giuliana quickly hops out of bed, puts on her favorite pink summer shorts and matching pink flowers blouse, then ties the laces of her shoes and hurries to the kitchen to have an early bowl of crunchy cereal and a glass of cold milk for breakfast. Believe it or not, timid, shy Karolina, holding and waving an adorable princess wand, is already sitting on the top step at the stoop in front of their house, waiting to start this new adventurous day. She is looking forward to, and hoping that she will be soon, on a colorful journey with her sister and friends. Giuliana carrying her sketchpad under her arm opens the front door to meet and greet her twin. She says, "Good morning, Karolina." Karolina replies, "I hope so! I didn't sleep much last night. I kept thinking, what is this groundhog's real name?" As she waves the princess wand back and forth in the fresh-morning air she says, "I keep wishing for the right answer." Giuliana puts her free arm around Karolina as she sits down on the top step next to her twin sister. Giuliana said, "Don't worry. I have this colorful journey under control. You'll see."

I walk up the steep, dead-end Jersey Street hill with our friends JoAnne, Rachel, Nancy, Dom, and my brother Peanut to meet the twins at their house. Junior rides his bike there, then parks it in the shade under the outstretched green-leaf-covered branches of the tall maple tree. Giuliana looks up and says, "Good morning, my good friends. Thanks for being here. Are you ready? Let's go!" With Giuliana carrying her sketchpad, Karolina waving her princess wand, all our friends gather at this starting point, and we all begin our journey up the winding footpath, expecting to meet the big, plump, fluffy, bossy groundhog.

The wild purple clover flowers that line the footpath on both sides are accompanied by delicate white long-stemmed Queen Ann's lace swaying in the morning breeze, yellow dandelions, and some that have turned to puffy white. An occasional busy bumblebee alights on the most beautiful wild yellow daisies and many orange and yellow honeysuckles that were clinging to a wild green-leafed bush. It is a delightful summer morning and lovely sweet-bird-chirping sounds filled the crystal-clear air. We walk to the exact spot that is designated by the groundhog to be our meeting place.

The beach-like soil here is quite sandy soft compared to the rest of the hard, dry-dirt surface with trees in this mountain meeting place. Perhaps that is why this area is referred to as the dried-out Morris Canal Bank. Many years ago, boats carrying products manufactured in north New Jersey traveled this Morris Canal water pathway east to markets in New York. I think, "Sandy soil in a north New Jersey mountain . . . Wow!" In the summer, I am used to traveling in Dad's 1957 green Plymouth station wagon on the Garden State Parkway south from Paterson to a soft sandy ocean beach at the Jersey Shore. The soil in this meeting place's exact spot where I am standing in Garret Mountain is as sandy soft as the ocean's sandy beach. Perhaps also, that is why every Sunday when the weather is nice, many men of Italian heritage play bocci here. Bocci is a game like bowling, but there are no pins to knock down and no bowling alleys. A small white ball (pallino) is the target on this sandy soil. The man who roll-throws a larger blue bocci ball closest to the white ball (pallino) scores a point. The team scoring the most points is the winning team. I wonder, "Did Pietro Botto play bocci here, in Garret Mountain, too?"

Wow! The water in the Morris Canal once flowed here. This water pathway has been dried out and now in the 1950s, metal train tracks have replaced the flowing water canal in this mountain. Locomotives travel quicker on this same path than slower boats traveled many years ago. I wonder, "*Hmmmm* ! Tomorrow, will these train tracks be removed and replaced by a super faster means to travel to the markets in New York?

We are all very quiet as we look around. We only wait a few seconds when over to our left side of the Morris Canal Bank, just at the first tier, the big, plump, fluffy, bossy groundhog's head pops out of a well-hidden hole in the rocky mountain. Immediately, the groundhog scampers over to meet us. Now, my heart begins pounding even faster than it is pounding when I walk up dead-end Jersey Street's steep hill with my friends to the winding footpath and the Morris Canal Bank. I am sure that I can hear the drumbeat pounding of my friends' hearts too. A few cute little rabbits, a deer, the red robin, and the blue dragonfly that we had met the day before stopped nearby to gaze at what is happening. The groundhog stands up on his hind legs to greet us. Sternly he says,

"Good morning!" He turns directly to Giuliana. He is right to the point when he calls out, "Well, I don't have all day! What's my real name?"

The drumbeat pounding stops for a second when we all hold our breath and our hearts stop beating. We all gasp! Then, Giuliana holds up the sketch that she drew of the groundhog and she replies, "Well . . . yesterday, when I was drawing this picture of you, my waxy crayons fell out of the cardboard crayon box. You promised us a colorful journey if I could guess your real name. I needed a crayon to color your furry coat." She holds the finished picture of the groundhog higher, and everyone gasps again at its likeness. The groundhog twitches his nose and scampers closer to Giuliana to get a better look at the picture. She hesitates then says, "The crayon that I chose for your beautiful furry coat was butternut-yellow." Suddenly, in the distance, a female groundhog's voice calls out, "Butternut! Butternut!" The groundhog looks up in amazement and says, "Ah! You got it!"

We all jump in the air, clap our hands, and hug each other, especially Giuliana. Then, Karolina spots a fluffy slightly reddish groundhog approaching our group of friends. This lady groundhog scampers over to stand next to Butternut. She wiggles her nose at us as she turns to look at Butternut. He says, "Please meet my wife, Magenta." Everyone calls out, "Hello, Magenta!" Butternut explains to his wife that he promised to take Giuliana and her friends on a colorful journey of Garret Mountain starting at the winding footpath if she would know his real name. He asks Magenta to please take the picture that Giuliana had so beautifully drawn of him and display it on a wall in their den. Magenta agrees. She takes the picture and begins to scamper off. "But wait!" He shouts to stop his wife. Then he says, "Giuliana, please autograph my picture." Giuliana takes her butternut yellow sketching pencil from out of her pocket and signs her work, the picture of Butternut. We all join Butternut in singing "Colorful Journey."

Colorful Journey
Colorful journey,
Come, everyone,
On a colorful journey,
Stick very close,
And follow the sun.

Two by two,
Me and you,
Red and orange,
Green and blue,

Colorful journey,
Lots of fun.

CHAPTER 5

It's for Real!

Butternut calls out, "Colorful journey! Are you ready?"

He gives the command, "Let's go! Stay close and listen up!" I don't have a wristwatch, so I figure as I look up at the orange-yellow sun still rising in the east and cotton-puff white cumulus clouds dotting the crystal-clear blue sky that it might be about 10:00 a.m. We start on our colorful journey of Garret Mountain with Butternut as our wonderful leader. A refreshing slight westerly breeze rustles the green leaf branches of the gigantic oaks and tall maple trees that tower over our heads in Garret Mountain. The evergreen trees point to the sky. There are bugs, black bugs, red bugs, brown bugs, bugs everywhere—crawling, flying, darting, buzzing, humming, and shy, timid Karolina is screaming, "A bee! A bee!" She begins swinging and swatting her adorable princess wand at every flying and crawling insect on the winding footpath, trying to make the swarming insect bugs disappear. *Swaaaaaat!*

The footpath is only a two-people wide passageway, so I pair up with JoAnne. Giuliana holds Karolina's wand-free hand. Nancy and Rachel walk together, and Peanut holds onto Dom's shoulder shirt sleeve. We cautiously follow Junior and our fearless leader Butternut. We carefully climb the first tier and look down at the sandy Morris Canal Bank and the shiny, smooth railroad tracks. Butternut warns us, "Be careful. Stop! Look! Listen! The Erie-Lackawanna train quickly passes here on those tracks several times a day. Watch your step when crossing the railroad tracks." Butternut makes it look so easy to get to the opposite side as he hops up, and leaps over the hot iron rails that line the tracks. Still waving her princess wand, shy Karolina softly repeats Butternut's warning, "Stop! Look! Listen!"

All I can think of is, "*Wooooooooooo!*" The sun seems to be getting much brighter and hotter. I am beginning to feel sticky sweaty. Following Butternut, we all run as quickly as we can up and over the hot iron railroad tracks trying to be very careful not to trip on the splintery hard wooden railroad ties. I notice an occasional railroad spike lying on the ground. I want to pick one up but think, "With this bright sun beating on the shiny metal, it might be too hot to touch." So, I don't. Then, not more than thirty seconds after we are across the railroad tracks and on the other side, we can feel the rumbling vibration in the solid earthy ground that we are standing on, hear a roaring thunderous sound getting louder every second, see big puffy dark-gray smoke rising in the air ahead of us. A huge locomotive is quickly heading in our direction. I begin to wonder, "Dark puffy gray smoke is swarming in the air! I am sure that right now, my mom and all the other ladies in our neighborhood are running outside to pull indoors the ringer washing machine clean wet clothes or the freshly handwashed wet clothes that are hanging outside to dry on the hard rope clotheslines that are attached to tall backyard trees! Hurry, moms!"

Karolina gently waves her princess wand in the smoky air as the rest of us wave to the engineer of the approaching train. The locomotive engineer toots the train's whistle three times, Toot! Toot! Toot! The engineer waves back to us with his hand.

Wooooooooooo! I had never before been this close to a moving locomotive.

Hmmmm! I wonder, "Was this locomotive engine manufactured in a factory at the Danforth-Cooke or the Rogers Locomotive Works on the corner of Spruce Street and Market Street in Paterson?"

Now, we are on the second tier of Garret Mountain. We are getting tired, so it is time to take a break and rest. Butternut begins to chomp on the small wildflowers growing near the railroad tracks. I can actually hear him chomping! Junior finds a huge granite rock that can accommodate all of us as a very, very hard seat. Giuliana immediately takes out her sketching pencils, waxy crayons, and her sketchpad to capture the surrounding colorful beauty of this experience. There is sparkling bright-pink feldspar, black mica, and dazzling white quartz running zigzag all through this hard, uncomfortable gigantic granite boulder that we are sitting on. Karolina says, "I'm thirsty!" I am so glad that someone has said something about thirst because I am about ready to mention it myself. JoAnne says, "I hear running water. Do you?" Butternut scampers over to a small crystal-clear puddle of fresh water that appears on the ground about ten feet away from our seat, the huge granite rock. He begins to lap up with his tongue as he drinks the crystal-clear water in the not-too-deep puddle.

A steady stream of water is flowing right out of a dark massive rock wall that has some soft green moss attached in this majestic mountain. Karolina, waving her princess wand calls out, "Spring water!" Then, disappointingly she says, "Great! Oh no! What do I use as a cup?" Junior holds her wand-free hand as he helps Karolina off the granite rock and walks with her to the overflowing water spring. He says, "Watch me." He cups his hands and places them under the spring's natural flowing spout to capture the cool, refreshingly cool, fresh spring water in his palms. Then Junior brings his cupped hands to his thirsty lips and drinks the sweet natural spring water. He says, "Now, you try this." Each of us takes turns in cupping our hands to take a drink and share the enjoyment of this cool refreshing rest stop. We are all captivated by the natural, colorful beauty of this journey. As I cup my hands, I can feel the coolness of this sparkling-fresh spring water slowly seeping through the tiny cracks between my adjoining fingers. The water drips to the ground as I sip. *Sssssssssssssssssssp!* So very, very refreshing!

Giuliana tucks her sketchpad under her arm, trying to keep it from getting wet with the splashing spray of the refreshing spring water. She cups her gifted, talented artist's hands and drinks the cool refreshing water!

All of a sudden, we can hear a rumbling, roaring, growling sound that seems to be coming from behind a huge pile of old broken dried-out tree branches that are lying on the ground about thirty feet from our granite-rock seat. Butternut immediately stops drinking and freezes in his spot. The growling grows louder and louder! *Rrrrrrrrrrrrrrrrrr*! Then, pointing with her wand, shy Karolina screams, "Look over there! What is that? Looks like a wild animal!" I say, "I can see his beady eyes!" Nancy shouts, "I think it's a fox!" Rachel calls out, "We must protect Butternut! Everybody, back up on the boulder and take Butternut with you." Immediately, JoAnne picks up Butternut, and we all run to the granite rock for protection. Dom very cautiously stoops down to pick up four palm-sized stones, and one at a time, he flings the stones in the direction of the green-leaf covered bushes near the brown-furred fox. Then, Junior and Peanut throw a few solid stones in the same direction. We can hear the rustle of the bushes' branches as the wild brown-coated fox hurriedly runs away from us. What a relief! Butternut, still in JoAnne's arms says, "Thanks, everyone. Thanks."

After we all capture our breaths, Butternut insists that we should continue on our colorful journey over the winding footpath and up to the third tier of this colorful Garret Mountain. I have to admit that after that encounter with the wild brown-coated fox, I lose some of my enthusiasm and courage concerning this expedition, but friends are friends and we must stick together. So, we pair off again climbing higher and higher over the rocky and wooded cliff territory. Now, I begin to hear a different kind of roar.

Rrrrrrrrrr! It is coming from my stomach, so I call out, "I'm hungry!"

Butternut hears my cry and leads us to an area where there are many trees of color. Huge tree branches hang nearly to the ground from the weight of the dangling ripe juicy red cherries, and bunches of blueberries begging to be picked. The handful of plump super deliciously sweet ripe blueberries that I eat makes my lips and tongue tint purple and blue. I just pick one red cherry at a time, pop it in my mouth, and spit out the pit.

Binggggg ! I must have eaten at least twenty sweet, delicious, ripe, juicy cherries from that beautiful cherry tree. We all agree. " Mmmmmmmmmmm!"

Looking at the sun's position in the sky, I figure that it is about 1:00 p.m. and we are still hiking on the winding footpath. I am thinking that my other friends are probably roller-skating or jumping rope on dead-end Jersey Street right now. Then, I hear shy Karolina gasp for breath and say, "Giuliana, Sweety, JoAnne, Nancy, Rachel . . . look . . . a castle!"

We can see this magnificent structure about one thousand feet straight ahead of us on the winding footpath. We all begin to wonder if a king and queen live here? The closer we get to this majestic castle, the bigger and bigger it appears. Giuliana, seizing the beauty of this amazing royal building, sits down on a puffy-green grassy knoll and opens her sketchpad. With solid-gray stone lions in front of huge arches guarding the massive castle's doors, Lambert Castle is amazing! We all run to gaze over the stone wall that surrounds the castle to overlook the city of Paterson below. I think, "The houses, trees, and cars look so little from way up here!" Butternut standing at the foot of the wall replies, "You're on the third tier." Then, it appears as though the sound of trumpets blares, ta . . . ta . . . ta ...ta . . . ta . . . ta . . . ta! We look around but see no trumpeters. Then, the drumbeat booms! Boom! Ba-boom! Boom! I wonder, "Where is this band music coming from?"

Facing the castle's main entrance, Karolina swiftly waves her princess wand in the air and like a piece of iron being pulled by a magnet, she is drawn to a most enchanting rose garden with four sandstone benches. Pink, red, yellow, lavender, and white blooming rosebushes border a mahogany-brick courtyard. A gentle breeze lifts the beautiful flowers' fragrance to surround and captivate us while we all sit on the solid sandstone benches to rest. As Karolina continues to wave her princess wand in the air, a twinkling, glittery light begins to sparkle beams that shoot out from under a beautiful lavender rosebush. Karolina bends down slightly to look under the rose petals to find the source of this twinkle. There, projecting from every fake gemstone on the brim is a glowing golden cardboard princess crown. Then a swift gusting breeze lifts the cardboard crown off the ground onto Karolina's head. Like magic, still holding her princess wand, suddenly Karolina begins to spin, twirl, skip, dance, and sing, "It's for Real."

It's for Real
It's for real, I feel, like a princess.
It's for real, I feel, like I'm royal, yes indeed.
It's for real, I feel, like a princess.
A wand and crown are all I'll ever need.
I'm so lucky that I found,
A colorful, majestic Garret Mountain with a crown.

We are all amazed to see the transformation that has taken place over our friend—timid, shy, frightened Karolina. Now, she is wearing a dazzlingly soft, glowing, golden cardboard crown and a beaming pink carnation smile on her face that glows with every dancing step and spin that she takes. She is indeed a radiant princess!

We are just about to begin heading home when walking out of the gigantic Lambert Castle doors, a very distinguished authoritative gentleman approaches us. At first, he stands with arms folded at the arch between the two solid-gray stone lions as he gazes at us. We are all amazed. Then this gentleman takes many giant steps in our direction to introduce himself, "I am Sir. Vincent of Paterson. Welcome! Visiting hours for this castle have just ended for today, but you may return tomorrow. Catholina Lambert, an English immigrant, owned a silk mill and made his fortune in the Paterson silk industry. He built this castle in Garret Mountain as a home for his wife and family in 1893. He called this castle home, Belle Vista. We call it, Lambert Castle."

Then he notices that Giuliana is sitting on the small puffy-green grassy knoll drawing in her sketchpad. As he takes giant steps walking over toward her, we follow. Giuliana looks up and apologetically says, "I'm very sorry if I should not be sitting here." Sir. Vincent replies, "You are perfectly welcome. What are you drawing?" Sir. Vincent stretches his neck to look over at Giuliana's drawing. Giuliana holds up a picture that she has just been creating of a lovely orange-red and black monarch butterfly that has posed for her as it sits on a lemon-yellow honeysuckle vine that is creeping up on the side of Lambert Castle's rock wall. Sir. Vincent responds to the drawing, "Colorful! Colorful! Colorful!" He replies, "I would like to invite you to visit Lambert Castle. Catholina Lambert was also an art collector. This castle houses a variety of very interesting artwork that I am sure you will love to see. Do you know of Gaetano Federici, Paterson's sculptor? Lambert Castle displays some of Federici's marvelous works. I can see that you are a very talented artist. Perhaps someday, one of your colorful artworks will be on exhibit here at Lambert Castle." Giuliana thanks Sir. Vincent for the compliment and assures him that someday she will return to visit Lambert Castle. We all just stand by in amazement! Butternut is hiding patiently under a yellow rosebush waiting for us.

Now the sun is beginning to glow down in the west. My stomach is roaring again as my biological clock is now ticking toward dinnertime and the chimes ring out, bong, bong, bong, bong! I figure it is about 4:00 p.m. Giuliana, Karolina, JoAnne, Nancy, Rachel, Junior, Peanut, Dom, and I gather to follow Butternut in a backtrack on the footpath as we descend this majestic Garret Mountain. Our shadows are behind us as the hot sun of the day is now creeping behind this colorful mountain. Holding onto each other, we carefully go down the third tier and descend to the second tier. Now, we need to cross the metal railroad tracks again to get to the first tier. When I examine the path of this railroad, it seems that those tracks extend west from New Jersey heading east to New York as far as my eyes could see. Butternut, Junior, Peanut, and Dom are many steps ahead of Giuliana, Karolina, JoAnne, Nancy, Rachel, and I.....Sweety. I must admit that although this colorful journey is full of excitement and fun, by this time of the day, I am dragging my tired feet.

The boys cross over the railroad tracks to the other side before us. Butternut is kind enough to wait for us staggering girls at the railroad crossing so we can all venture over the tracks together. Just as Giuliana, Karolina, JoAnne, Nancy, Rachel, and I begin stepping over the splintery wooden railroad ties, we feel the vibration of another oncoming train. Karolina waving her wand, yells to us, "Hurry!" Then she turns to the butternut-yellow groundhog and calls out, "Butternut! Hurry!" We can hear the train's loud whistle and feel the trembling vibrations at our feet became more intense as it travels throughout our bodies. We run and jump as fast as we can over the shiny metal railroad tracks to the other side. Giuliana exhaustingly calls out,

"We . . . just . . . made . . . it!" Karolina quickly looks around and shouts, "Where is Butternut? Butternut! Butternut!" The loud rumble echoes from the passing locomotive engine with too many cars for us to count. Finally, there is the caboose and the thunderous, roaring train sound beginning to fade. We look around, wondering, "Where is Butternut?"

Happy thoughts do not enter my mind. The horror of the possibility that Butternut may not have made it safely across the railroad tracks in time gives me a horrible feeling and more quivering shakes. Then, Karolina waves her princess wand in the air. A small head with two glassy eyes peers out from under the center of the railroad tracks. Karolina loudly cries out as she points her wand, "Butternut!" Rachel says, "Is he moving?" Within seconds that big, plump, fluffy, bossy groundhog jumps out from under the rails and scampers down the railroad tracks to meet us. We all take turns in hugging him. Butternut responds, "Don't let my name, Butternut Yellow, fool you. I am not a yellow coward!" He assures us that this is not his first encounter with a moving locomotive at these tracks in this mountain.

From here, the backtrack walk on the winding footpath is only a few hundred feet to the sandy Morris Canal Bank where Magenta, Butternut's beautiful wife, has been waiting for her husband's return. Each of us: Giuliana, Karolina, JoAnne, Nancy, Rachel, Junior, Peanut, Dom, and I.....Sweety thank courageous Butternut Yellow for leading us on this wonderful, colorful journey. Butternut thanks us for being his friends, and then he scampers off with his wife to his territory, his den, in his colorful majestic Garret Mountain.

At the foot of Garret Mountain, on dead-end Jersey Street, our friends Leon, John-John, and Cathy are sitting under the shade of the maple tree in front of Giuliana and Karolina's house waiting for us to return. Leon says to the boys, "You were gone all day! It was impossible to play flag football without you." John-John says, "We couldn't play stickball either!" Cathy calls to Giuliana, "Did you know the groundhog's real name? Tell us about your happening!" So, as Karolina and I find a spot to sit and rest at the stoop on the steps with all our friends, Giuliana, the artist, opens her sketchpad. One at a time, she releases her drawings that tell the story of the wonderful, colorful journey we took on the winding footpath in this colorful, majestic Garret Mountain with a courageous leader groundhog friend named, Butternut Yellow.

As I am sitting next to Karolina, looking up at the three tiers in this colorful, majestic Garret Mountain, I continue to wonder, "When George Washington, Alexander Hamilton, Marquis de Lafayette or Pierre L'Enfant galloped on their horses to visit the great flowing river waterfalls to make industrial plans for this new country, did they also visit here? Did they walk on a colorful journey taking the same vibrant footpath that Butternut Yellow led us on today in this colorful majestic mountain? Did they see the beautiful flowers, hear the chirping birds, or meet any wild animals? Did they rest on the same hard granite rock and drink sparkling spring water from the same cool, refreshing natural watering spring? Wow! They were here, in this Paterson, New Jersey area approximately two hundred years ago. This is the 1950s. Did this colorful, majestic Garret Mountain change since they visited here? I am sure that there was no Jersey Street, Lambert Castle, or locomotives that traveled on train tracks here in the 1700s. How different was Garret Mountain when immigrants came to work in Paterson's factories and mills in the 1800s?

Wow! I wonder! What will the future be for Paterson's great waterfalls, dead-end Jersey Street, and this colorful majestic Garret Mountain? How will we travel on a colorful journey here in the next century? Wow!"

Colorful Journey..... Crossword Puzzle Questions

Across:

2. Who hangs wet washed clothes on a clothesline to dry?
3. Industrial Workers of the World
5. What is the groundhog's real name?
7. What do they pick off the trees to eat?
9. What is Karolina holding and waving?
10. What is the name of the mountain?
12. Who's house did the Industrial Workers of the World union leaders speak from on the second floor balcony?
13. What is the name of the castle?
14. What do they meet at the spring?
16. What is another name for a hot factory?

Down:

1. Giuliana is a wonderful_____.
2. What is the name of the canal that flowed across the mountain?
4. Who spent much time in the vicinity of the Passaic River near his headquarters at the Dye Mansion in Preakness Valley/ Wayne, New Jersey?
6. What travels on tracks through the mountain?
8. What do the boys use as a bat to play stickball?
9. What do they drink at the spring?
10. Who ate lunch with George Washington at the massive great waterfalls in the 1700s.
14. What is the sound that the train's whistle made?

Colorful Journey..... Crossword Puzzle

Colorful Journey..... Crossword Puzzle Answers

Across / Down entries:

- ³I ⁴W W
- ¹A / ²M O M
- R / O
- A S / ⁵B U T T E R N U T / ⁶T
- I / R / R
- ⁷C H E R R I E S / I / A
- I / T / S / I
- N / ⁸B / ⁹W A N D
- ¹⁰G A R R E T / A
- T / O / T
- ¹²B O T T O M / ¹¹H / R / ¹⁴T
- N / M / ¹³L A M B E R T / O
- A / ¹⁵F O X
- I / T
- L
- T
- ¹⁶S W E A T S H O P
- N